THE HIDING HOUSE

Story and Pictures by
Judith Vigna

Albert Whitman & Company, Chicago

Copyright © 1979 by Judith Vigna
Published simultaneously in Canada
by General Publishing, Limited, Toronto
All rights reserved. Printed in U.S.A.

Library of Congress Cataloging in Publication Data

Vigna, Judith.
    The hiding house.

    (A Concept book)
    SUMMARY: The exclusive nature of Marybeth and Bar-
bara's friendship is challenged when a new girl moves
into their neighborhood.
    [1. Friendship—Fiction]   I. Title.
PZ7.V67Hi   [E]   79-17251
ISBN 0-8075-3275-4

I'm Marybeth, and this is my best friend, Barbara.

We do everything together.

We paint.

We dress up.

We go to the candy store
and drink chocolate shakes
with a double squirt of
whipped cream on top.

NAILS

We even have our own house.
It was an old shed in my backyard.
Barbara's father helped us fix it up.

We call it the Hiding House.
We go there when we don't
want anyone to bother us.

We hung some curtains
and put up our paintings.

Sometimes, when it's warm,
our parents let us sleep there.

We take milk and brownies
so we won't starve during
the night.

Nobody's allowed inside
the Hiding House.

Not even my brother and sister.

Barbara said it would be okay
to let them in,
but I said NO.

It's OUR house and I don't want them.

If anyone tries to come in,
we put on our most fierce and
horrible masks
and yell and scream
until we scare them away.

Once, when the moon was big,
we built a pile of magic stones
and made an oath.

The two of us will be best friends
until we die.

The other day, a huge van
stopped outside the house
next to Barbara's.

Some people started to move
a whole load of stuff through
the front door.

Then a car drove up,
and a little girl climbed out.

Barbara went over to talk to her.
"Hello, I'm Barbara," she said.

"I hope you'll be my friend.
Marybeth and I have a Hiding House
and you can come over any time you want."

I was ANGRY.

I was SO angry I made up
my mind never to let Barbara
into the Hiding House again.

Even if she banged on the door
until it broke into
a million
splinters!

I heard her call,
"Marybeth! Marybeth! Let me in!"

But I didn't answer.
Finally she went away.

After hours and hours and hours
everything got quiet and spooky…

...so I opened the window,
just a tiny bit, and looked out.

Barbara and Jill were outside.
I heard Barbara say,
"I must have done something
terrible. Marybeth
always said I was
her BEST FRIEND!"

"Barbara, wait!" I shouted.

"You ARE my best friend!"

"And if Jill wants to come
into the Hiding House,
that's okay,
sort of."

Now I have another best friend...

and Barbara doesn't mind at all.